BIG BODY BASE II

BIG BODY BASE II

Cover Design By: © Inakat Graphic Designs

BIG BODY BASE II

Dedication

This book is dedicated to my brother Mr. Charles M. Thomas, Detroit's own DJ Base (The Mixologist). He has selflessly shared his passion and gifts of music through education of Detroit City youth. He has been an active role model, friend, father figure, and inspiration to many, including myself. Well known for his sense of humor and positive words, and even tough love when needed, Mr. Thomas continues to inspire me never to give up on my passion for writing. For that, I will forever be grateful.

Inakat

"We do not stop" #4life

BIG BODY BASE II

BIG BODY BASE II

Table of Contents

BIG BODY BASE II

CHAPTER ONE

"Get that thing out of my face, Misty," Thomas said.

"Just act natural Mr. Movie Star." Misty teased.

"I'm not playing girl, go somewhere with that thing."

"What you gone do? If you touch me, I'm telling mama."

"If I get up from this table, you won't tell a soul when I let you go little girl. Ain't you supposed to be getting dressed for school anyway?"

"Nope, got kicked out. I can't go back until Thursday when mama takes me back to a conference."

"She just took you back last week. What did you get kicked out for this time?"

"Fighting, what else."

"Why? You stress the hell out of mama. Why are so damn mean? You're too smart for that."

"I didn't do anything to that girl. I am not going to stand there and let people push me around. If you hit me, then you must want to fight. She punched me in the arm first. Mr. Weatherly act as if he can't see anything. I told her to stop, and she did it again. I got up and smashed her in the face with my World History book. He saw me hit her and put me out. Then Mrs. Crawford called the house and told mama I couldn't come back until Thursday."

"I don't understand how you managed to pass to the next grade. You stay put out more than you are in class. You should only be like in the second grade. Cut that thing off Misty."

"Mama called you."

"Sit your little bad ass down somewhere."

"I'ma tell you cussing."

"I'ma give you something to tell if you don't get that thing out of my face. The house is going to be good and clean by Thursday. Mama is not about to let you run around and play all day. You are gone to clean the baseboards with a toothbrush, pick the carpet clean with tweezers, and get the dust bunnies from under the water tank with a feather. Now, was hitting that girl back worth it?"

"Yep"

Thomas rolled his eyes at his sister as he got up from the table. He cleared away his dishes before he went to the front door. Misty backed up with the camera, and then followed him. She caught the look on Thomas's face when he saw his company.

Thirty students stood lined up in the field on Spruce Street. Thomas's mouth fell open when he saw the kids. Slowly, he opened the screen door and gawked at the crowd. The section leaders were the older kids, and they appeared to have the new recruits in order. When they saw Thomas, one of them yelled.

"Okay, let's show our director what we got guys!"

CHAPTER TWO

Misty had barely made pulled up from her drive from Michigan when she, at last, broke down in tears. She felt as if she failed in her attempt to be there for someone that she loved. She was disappointed that her ex-husband had continued to use the children as pawns and even more discouraged that the children did not yet see it.

The children were adults now. She could only hope that she had given them the tools they needed to survive the harsh realities of life. Although they had been extremely cruel, she wished them happiness. There was not much to for her to do about it, besides, play the hand she had been dealt and move on with her life. Misty pulled her nerves together and strengthened her resolve while she parked her car.

The sun had begun to rise over the sleepy small town. As the night shadows rolled back to give way to day, Misty rifled through her purse for tissues and the keys to her door. Once she found the keys, she sniffled, got out of the car, and headed towards the gate. Fresh tears rolled while she placed the key in the lock. The door swung open with a loud bang. She went in. Misty quickly opened the blinds to let sunlight come in.

She had only made it as far as the kitchen when her house phone rang. She looked at the caller ID. It was her father. Misty decided to get her coffee before she took any calls. She flitted around the kitchen while she prepared her favorite morning beverage.

Fifteen minutes later, Misty called her father. She let him know that she had arrived safely. James told her he was glad that she was safe. Misty told her dad that she loved him and hung up. Her hand rested on the cradle on the phone briefly and she sighed.

She went into the kitchen, poured a cup of fresh hot coffee, and took it to the contemporary sofa with her. Misty kicked off her shoes, sat on the couch, and sipped her hot, steamy drink. She missed her family already. The hardest part about the visits to her was when she left. Misty took the cup and sat it on the coffee table.

Usually, when she had moments like this, Misty would take out the tapes of her family and watch them. It made her feel better to see them. The ones of her mother were ones that she had not been able to watch very much. She got up and sauntered over to the cabinet where she kept the tapes.

She ran her index finger over the labels. It was not long before she found one that made her smile. She pulled the tape from its slot and walked it over to the VCR. Misty slipped the tape into the machine and poked the power button on the television and then the VCR. She went back to the couch, sat down, and immediately burst into the giggles.

The screen had come alive with a sight she could remember very clearly. She had filmed it years ago. It was footage of an early morning in the Base household. Misty continued to smile while the tape played.

A much younger Thomas ate breakfast at the kitchen table in their family home. He rushed through a Danish and juice. He had worked two jobs and always seemed to be on the go to Misty. More often than not, Thomas struggled to the house in the wee hours, showered, fell asleep on the couch or in the Lazy boy recliner for a few hours. Then woke up pumped and on the go.

The video scene before her now was a special moment, though. Thomas had recruited a new batch of the sixth graders at his school into the band at Pelham. They wanted to learn band music very much. Daylight had just begun to break when they showed up at the house.

Misty could hear herself laugh, as her mother yelled that Thomas had company from the front porch. Misty's mom usually had her coffee on the front porch every day while the sun came up. She had once explained it to Misty that it was her quiet time with the Lord. When she took a moment to thank him for another day and pray for her family and friends.

Misty had not planned to get the footage that she had. The year before on her birthday, her parents had bought her a used camcorder front a local pawn shop. She had not hesitated to use it to annoy her big brother every chance she got. That morning was no exception while she followed him around the house and recorded him.

Without instruments, at the break of dawn, the students followed the hand commands of the each section leader. They marched out and formed a star, then marched back into their previous lines. Thomas smiled. The same student that had had called out to his band mates to start had played the role of Thomas, as he stood aside and looked on. Several quick shrills from a whistle called for complete attention. The student in charge then made a waving motion and the mini-band turned and marched towards the house.

They all stopped short of the sidewalk, and near the edge of the street. The mini-Thomas then turned and gave a different signal. The children roared, "Because of you, we rock!" They then gave a military-style salute and turned away from Thomas. They marched up the street towards the school in a neat and organized manner.

Thomas burst out with laughter and slapped his thigh. When after about forty steps, someone from the group had begun to beat-box the tune of "Ain't no mountain high enough". The children continued their public step-show styled March and the clapped the parts of the instruments. Thomas wiped a tear from his eye while his laughter resonated the passionate love that he had always had for teaching music.

"That's some tribute Mr. Thomas," Mama said.

"Them kids, oh wow, them kids..." Thomas replied.

"They love you for what you do. Look at your little mini-me. Looks just like you mocking Mr. Love don't it. Bet you didn't see this coming did you?"

"No Ma, I didn't. This is too funny, though."

"Yep, keep up the good work son. Just keep on doing what you are doing."

"Yes, ma'am. I have got to get out of here and get to the school. Them kids ain't got no business up at that school this time of morning alone."

"See, that's why they did that. They know that you genuinely care. Gone boy, gone 'head, and get out of here. Love you baby."

"Love you too Ma."

Thomas reached for the screen door. He paused, turned and bent down, and kissed Mama on her cheek. She giggled and showed him on. Thomas went inside to get dressed.

About fifteen minutes later, Thomas barreled out the house. He shouted his goodbyes while he sprinted to his white Dodge Horizon to warm it up. Misty recorded him as his car pulled off from the window. She watched as Thomas's car drove up Spruce and turned left up Vermont, with her camcorder in hand. Until she could no longer see her big brother, Misty stayed in that spot.

CHAPTER THREE

Misty held her side. She had held in her laughter so long that it had begun to pain her. She often wondered why Thomas put up with her as a child, without stuffing her in a cabinet. Most siblings fought like animals where they were from. However, Thomas had restrained from things most brothers did for fun to their little sisters. He usually kept a smile on her face.

She had known that she had been somewhat of a pest to him. His size meant that he could swat her like a fly at any time, yet he did not. They were worlds apart in nature but close at heart. She admired him, and he doted on her.

Thomas had hired her at first real job at the Burger Shack, where he was a manager at night. Misty thought that she would be able to continue her silly ways at the job. Thomas wanted her to learn some personal responsibility. He had done her the favor of guided experience in the real world, by giving her a chance.

Thomas had given out the assignments for the evening crew. Misty had been on the sandwich prep line for two months. He needed to be able to move around to other stations. He told her to go and mop the lobby and Misty scoffed.

"Misty, we're not at home. Everyone has to take their turn to wash the lobby and clean the bathrooms." Thomas said.

"I don't mop the floor at home unless I'm in trouble for something. Do I get to punch somebody in the face first? It's a couple of them that could use a quick backhand." Misty said.

"That's not the point. The point is I asked you as an employee of Burger Shack, to mop the floor."

"I told you, I don't mop the floor at home."

"Okay, you can clock out, and that is where you can go. Go back, Misty."

"Yep"

Misty stomped off to the time clock. She punched out, left the restaurant, and went straight home. She was angry with him. Misty waited up until Thomas came home that night. As soon as she heard him opened the door, she confronted him.

"Why you send me home in front of all those people?" Misty asked.

"The same reason you disobeyed me in front of all those people Misty. I love you, but if I stood there and let you tell me that you were not going to do your job, it's not fair to everyone else. I can't treat you special because you're my sister. It was a challenge to get you in there. I can't believe that you clowned me like that. I am dog-tired, and I have to get up in a few hours. You wanted to make money. Do my laundry and I'll pay you, but you're not coming back to Burger Shack."

Misty put her down and frowned. Her cheeks began to burn. She had not intended for Thomas to be upset with her. She knew what she had to do.

"Sorry," Misty mumbled.

"What?" Thomas said.

"I told you i apologize, Thomas."

"Oh, I thought I heard you say you were sorry. I accept your apology. I refuse that accept that you are sorry. I do not have any sad ass sisters. Don't let me hear you say that again."

"Okay"

"Now take your ass to bed. You can't stay woke in class, but you can stay awake to front somebody when you're wrong."

"You mad at me?"

"I'm disappointed at what you did. Mad don't help you or me. You got that Base family temper. You have to learn when and where to let it go. There's a time and place for things Misty, at work, it wasn't the time or the place to think I was playing with you."

"I still love you too."

"That's what's up, now go to bed before Mama come through here and catch you."

Misty eyes got wide. She rushed into her bedroom and flopped on the bed. The mention of their mother had been a real threat after the last conference at the school. Her mother had made it plain that if Misty got into any more trouble at school, she was going to get a beating.

Misty had spent a good third of her childhood life on punishment. Her mother usually gave extra chores out as a chastisement of her children, but she was not beyond a swift chop to the throat right where one stood. That included but was not limited to church, the supermarket, school, the mall, or in front of friends. Her mother's philosophy was that if you could embarrass her, surely you could not be too surprised when she returned the favor.

Misty came to herself in the front room of her house and resolved to continue her day with a smile. The tape had stopped. Misty stood up and stretched. She picked up her cup and took it to the sink. Misty chuckled to herself from the events on the tape.

CHAPTER FOUR

Misty decided to shower before she went back out to get her bags from the car. A half-hour later, a refreshed Misty emerged from a steamed-filled bathroom. She had decided to air dry, as she put on her body lotion. Except for slippers, she wore only her birthday suit. Misty went into her bedroom and tried to decide which lotion she wanted to use.

Misty had just bent over to read the labels when she heard a soft knock on her front door. She reached behind the bedroom door and pulled down a housecoat. She wrapped the satiny fabric around her still damp body. Misty walked left her room, went to the front door, and peeked through the small window. She saw someone who had their head turned toward the street and unlocked the door.

"Can I help you?" Misty asked.

The man on the porch turned around. Misty hand went up to her throat. He was gorgeous. He smiled at Misty and held out a package.

"Misty Base?" He asked.

"Yes," Misty said.

"I have a package for you. It requires a signature."

Misty did not move as the man extended the pen for her to sign. She swallowed hard and blinked several times. She wanted to move, take the pen, and sign for her package. Misty found herself unable to move a muscle. It felt as if her knees were about to give.

"Are you okay?" the man asked.

"Yes, I apologize," Misty said.

Misty extended her hand and reached out for the pen. He looked down at her hand and saw it trembled badly. She wondered if he noticed. At last, she managed to steady her hand enough to take the pen.

She scribbled her name on the tablet that he had given her. In her haste, Misty had forgotten to tie her robe closed. When the man passed her the small cardboard box, she reached out to get it. Her wrap parted. He held the box in mid-air and paused.

"Ummm...I don't know if you know, but I can see...stuff." He said.

Misty felt the tip of both of her ears get hot. She scrambled to close her housecoat quickly. She turned her head away from him and reached for the box again. She felt it touch her fingers and latched onto it while she avoided eye contact with him. Misty was slightly embarrassed.

"Thank you, Ms. Base. Thank you very much. Or is it Mrs. Base?" He asked.

"It's Ms. Base," Misty replied.

"Even better, now I won't feel sorry about that mental picture I just took for later."

"I didn't intend to..."

"I understand. You've probably got a jealous boyfriend somewhere that would be very upset."

"No. It was an accident. I just finished my shower when you came. I forgot to tie this thing up so when I reached…it was an accident."

"That was the best accident I've had in my life. So no boyfriend, husband, or significant other in your life at this time. Is okay if I ask for how long?"

"Two years."

"Is that so? At the risk of rejection, would you like to go out sometime?"

"Maybe…"

"How about I swing back through when I get off, and we can talk about it?"

Misty finally looked at him and smiled. She shrugged her shoulder as if she was indifferent. He raised one eyebrow and smiled back at her. Misty shyly pulled the box to her chest.

"My name is Kaiden Jedrek; it's a pleasure to meet you Misty," Kaiden said.

"It's nice to meet you too Kaiden," Misty said.

"See you later?"

"See you later."

Misty closed the door slowly. She peeked out the window and watched while Kaiden made his way back to his truck. His broad shoulders rippled under his uniform jacket. When he turned to see if she was still there, she ducked down and put her hand over her mouth. Misty slid down to the floor and giggled.

"Did I just make a date with him?" Misty asked aloud.

She rose up and ran to her room. Misty dove across the bed and shrieked. He was her definition of super fine. She took a pillow from the top of the bed and covered her face in the midst of a silly moment. Misty mock smothered herself for a second while she laughed and kicked her legs in the air.

Kaiden had dark mocha colored eyes that made him look youthful. His precise tapered fade accented his incredible sharp jaw line. Kaiden seemed like he was the type that was most comfortable in pressed jeans and a casual shirt to Misty. Maybe even fatigues and boots, but something that he could relax in. He stood about five foot seven with a solid body.

After a few moments, Misty composed herself and sat up. Her shoulders heaved as reality set. Her tummy balled up in a knot. It had been a habit to act before she thought in the area of relationships. Kaiden was attractive, but Misty had vowed to keep a level head and stay single for a while.

As much as she despised the individual life at times, she had stayed single for a reason. Misty wanted a particular type of mate. However, she had yet to define what was special to her. Besides, Misty had not actively sought anything more than the occasional company, in months. After a messy divorce, a friend turned lover, and then a longtime partner turned friend, Misty quit dating.

Misty liked to spend time alone. It was a personal choice. More often than not, she was able to blend into a crowd and mingle. It was in the privacy of her mind where she found the most comfort. She had reasoned that sex was something she could handle on her own. Lately, her body had more than suggested that it disagreed. Like the moment at the door with Kaiden.

Kaiden had given her something new to contemplate. Misty felt she could keep it casual. She had managed to do so in the past. She had fiercely guarded her heart and kept an emotional distance from dates. Misty was confident that an appointment with Kaiden could be fun and simple.

She immediately ran through her mental list to keep her emotional meter in check. Misty believed that she finally learned to be in total control of her heart. She would be calm, cordial, and demure. Still, if there was any chemistry between she was sure she could walk away without a commitment. Then Misty realized that the pillow had made its way between her thighs and rolled over.

CHAPTER FIVE

Kaiden was a peaceful, relaxed, easy-going person, for the most part. However, when riled his temper is evident. He did not usually lash out at women. After he had found the last girlfriend in bed with someone else, he had broken off the relationship without much conversation.

Kaiden let it burn, inside him, though. His ex-girlfriend was a co-worker than he had to see briefly in the warehouse a few days a week. Since the incident, whenever he saw her his conversations with her were both brief and slightly sarcastic. He became amazingly motivated to flirt with other women in front of her. The women teased back too. However, Kaiden wanted to move on and find someone to fill the void in his life forever, not just a quickie.

Kaiden grew up in the south, and both of his parents had a strong side. Much like Misty, he had come from a loving family. He connected with both parents and attempted to blend in each of the two personalities into his own. As a man, Kaiden had not quite found a way to express himself. He could not bring himself to tell his ex how he felt and to be done with it.

He spent a good deal of time on the inner battle more than on the outside task. He had had many different jobs, drove a pristine late model Chevy Impala, and occasionally went to strip clubs. His routine had been his downfall with women. Kaiden has recently given up on the seedy nightlife and spent more time alone. He was determined, not to be lured by just another beautiful face again.

He wanted a woman that had it all. Sex appeal was high on his list, but she also had to be smart and witty. A woman on her own, strong and beautiful, yet carefree and seductive. Someone he could share the wealth of life.

Kaiden had been accommodating but complacent in his relationships. While women felt calm around his peacefulness, they became irritated that he was not direct with his wants. He had been attracted to women that were submissive in nature. Lately, he found that he preferred women that were a little more aggressive.

Kaiden had spent a lot of time with his grandparents as a child. His mother was a physician that often traveled out of the country to bring Healthcare to nations struck with tragedy. His father worked at the local post-office. Their schedules made it difficult to get much quality time with either of his parents.

His grandmother had spent hours with him. She had imparted much wisdom to him but rarely spoke to him about relationships. Often she used the Bible as a reference point for any questions about love. She had done so with the best of intentions; however, it left Kaiden without the ability to separate righteousness from just right.

He found Misty attractive. Before he walked off the porch, he already decided that he would pursue her. He smiled as he remembered her buoyant breasts and dark brown skin peek from under her satin housecoat. She met the first qualifications, which were sexy and shapely.

Kaiden smirked as he parked his delivery truck in front of his stop. He visited an address at least once every few weeks. He had come to her home many times as a teenager with his grandfather. The woman often ordered packages from EBay.

He had spent a weekend with her once in his late teens. His grandfather had to have a minor surgery in Chicago. His grandparents had left him with the grandmotherly neighbor Mrs. Silver in their absence. It had become one of the most memorable weekends of his life.

Kaiden had slept on her couch. Like most teenage boys he had awakened aroused. He heard the woman in the kitchen. She recited some poetry as she clinked around in the kitchen to prepare breakfast. He wrapped himself in the cover she had given him the night before, stood up, and tried to walk past the kitchen door with his head down.

"Good morning young man." Mrs. Silver shouted.

"Morning," Kaiden said.

Before he could reach the bathroom door, Mrs. Silver stepped out in front of him. In his haste and with his head down, Kaiden's face rammed into the cavern of her ample bosom. He stepped backward but not before; he had inhaled the sweet Lavender aroma from her skin. The urge to push her to get to privacy overwhelmed him.

"Why you all wrapped up like a mummy? You are dragging one of my good sheets across the floor. I'll turn on the heat if you're cold but you have to put that sheet back on the couch now." Mrs. Silver said.

"I'm not cold, and it's just…" Kaiden stuttered.

"It's just what. You got wood this morning. Woke up with a nice firm stiffy, did you?"

"Umm…I would rather not discuss stuff like that with you Mrs. Silver, no disrespect."

"It's disrespectful to hide that lovely boner from a mature woman. What do you think I have not seen one before? Are You going to the bathroom to tug off, huh? What a waste. You should find yourself a hot little number to lay that too. Your granddaddy hasn't taken you down to the Birdcage. I used to work there a long time ago. Back before I married Mr. Silver. That man got a boner sometimes four times a day, until he died. That is why I married him. He spent so much time and money at the club in my room that I just packed my bags one weekend and left with him."

"What's the Birdcage? A strip club or something?"

"The Birdcage is a brothel. I used to be a Madame there."

"You used to sell your body, Mrs. Silver? Wow."

"What the hell is wrong with you boy? You think I am supposed to give it away. There is nothing worse than a woman coming home with a wet ass and dry purse. Some men would rather not pay for dinner and a movie when all they want is to relieve a boner. In that case, they reduce the art of lovemaking down to sex. No frills or thrills. Some women have no interest in listening to a man drone on about how pretty she is just to get into her panties. She wants a real time. There is no guarantee sex is going to be a good time. Peel off some crispies to her and one out of two isn't such a bad compromise. I can always have fun shopping."

"Strippers have sex for money?"

"Not all of them. Not all hookers strip and all strippers ain't hookers. Your mom stripped her way to a degree. Couldn't pay her for nothing but a look. The way your poor father seems most of the time, apparently she found a client that paid so often he got chose. That's life boy. To the victor go the spoils."

"That's disgusting Mrs. Silver."

"You got any pictures of women that get you going? A stash of nudie pics or a magazine or two with doves that get your dandruff going?"

Kaiden blushed. His eyes wandered to the floor. He had a collection of photos that he had taken from his grandfathers old Playboy magazines that were in the trash. He had carefully cut out the ones that he found the most attractive and kept. On a few occasions, he and a few friends had given the town drunk a few quarters to purchase adult magazines for them. Afterward, he had discarded the books.

"A few" Kaiden admitted.

"Do you think those women took money to pose in their underwear or birthday suits or do it stand to reason that they got paid first, and you're the one that paid for it?" Mrs. Silver said.

"I didn't pay them to do anything. They were already naked when I bought the book."

"Now is that what you think? You got a lot to learn sonny. Somebody paid them first to get naked and take the pictures. That same somebody was probably a horny young man that was willing to pay to see naked women. He figured out that if he were willing to pay, then he could probably sell them too. He paid the women first. Then recouped his with money with what you paid for his collection of nudes. So whether you like the idea or not, you paid for it. Because you did, it in private doesn't change anything. No doubt if the woman was a soiled dove and you found her attractive, you would pay actually to do some of the stuff you thought about while you tugged on your little steamboat on the toilet and gawked at her boobies."

"I wouldn't do that Mrs. Silver."

"Look here young man, my husband been dead for seven years. If a man comes to my door to make a deal, I am not going to turn him away. I don't judge anybody, but if you can buy a nudie picture you oughts' to be able to buy a little of the real thing. It ain't tricking, if you got it."

"Any man Mrs. Silver?"

"You got any of that paper route money saved up? Better, get on in the bathroom and handle up yourself. When you get tired of those hand jobs, break open that stash of cash, come on, and see me sometimes. Wash your hands and come to the table for breakfast."

"I wasn't going to do that."

"Sure you weren't, that's why you tried to hide that boner."

CHAPTER SIX

As a grown man, Kaiden recalled the time that Mrs. Silver had offered him her services. She was, at least, fifty years older than he was back then. Since that time, she had lost most of her hair save a few scraggly patches on the sides, all of her teeth, and suffered a stroke that left her housebound. It was at that time that he heard the rumors that she had been a smack addict too. It would take her nearly twenty minutes to get to the door with the aid of a walker.

Kaiden quickly jogged up the stairs to her down, opened the screen, put the small box inside, and rang her bell. He had begun to sign for her packages as a favor to her. Her handwriting was now a scrawled line that was unreadable because of her illness. He had not ever gone to her for the favors that she had offered him. Kaiden had however visited a place much like the Birdcage once, because of her story.

He had taken his time to choose a partner. Once he had, his money had barely left his pocket before he had an orgasm. The woman hurried him out of the room as she rinsed her mouth. Kaiden found himself out in the lobby just as quickly as he had entered the room.

After that, he concluded that he didn't mind having to pay for attention. He didn't like confrontation. He had managed to reduce his sexual encounters to a quick romp for hire. Meanwhile, his immediate needs were taken care of, but he had not learned how to interact with women. His conversations included words like "must" and "shall. Most women found it a complete turn-off.

His latest ex-girlfriend had taken advantage of him. Kaiden told her about his desire to have an exclusive relationship with her. When he dropped by her place, he noticed the two cars parked in her driveway. He parked his car, got out, and knocked on the door. The hot summer sun beamed down on him while he made his way to the porch.

A few moments passed, and no one responded. Kaiden walked off the porch and headed towards the backyard. As he passed a bedroom window on the side of her home, he paused. Through the sheer curtains, Kaiden saw her. She was not alone.

Two men sat off the foot of her bed. They were undressed from the waist down. Kaiden cringed when he saw her come into his view. She wore a bra and panties. When she stood in front of one of the men then dropped to her knees, Kaiden walked away.

Kaiden had enjoyed a fair amount of wild sex with her. Still, he had specifically asked that she reserve herself for him only. After he had caught her in the act, he simply walked away from her. His face twisted as he clenched his teeth. That blowjob was his, and she gave it to someone else.

It was late in the evening when she called him at home. Kaiden answered the phone. He listened as she asked sweetly about his day. He slammed the phone down. She called right back, and he answered again.

"I think we got disconnected, Kaiden," She said.

"No, I hung up on you. I came by today. Who were those guys at your house?" Kaiden asked.

"Oh…umm. Those were some of the guys from the choir, the organist, and drummer."

"So what you play the skin flute now. I did not know that was choir position. I wanted to marry you, and you've ruined it."

"I don't know what you're talking about."

"I saw you."

"I'm sorry. It was a moment of weakness. It won't ever happen again."

"I don't care if it does. There has to be a decent woman worth the effort. You can play the skin flute for the piano man while the drummer puts his sticks in your sloppy box. Let me ask you something, did either one of them leave you a few dollars for your time?"

"What? No, I am not a prostitute. It wasn't like that."

"Yeah sweetheart, kick rocks. I do not want a woman in my life that sleeps with other men and does it free. You should have gotten a little silver, gold, or green in the process."

"I made a mistake. If this is a relationship then why can't we work this out?"

"I can't turn a hoe into a housewife. In fact, I don't want to."

"I'm coming over there so we can talk about this Kaiden."

He slammed the phone down again. Kaiden had gone home to relax after he seen her with those men. He sat on his rust colored micro-fiber sofa to watch television. After he had hung up on her, Kaiden picked up the remote from the coffee table and turned up the television.

An hour later, he heard a knock on his front door. Kaiden looked at it. He remained seated. The knocks resumed louder and more frequent. Kaiden with remote still in hand turned up the volume on his television until he could no longer hear anything but the television.

CHAPTER SEVEN

Misty eventually made herself get off the bed and get into fresh clothes. She chose a simple striped tube dress that clung to her curves. She walked into the living room barefoot and paused. The tape had turned itself back on somehow. Thomas's brilliant smile flashed across the screen.

She strolled over to the set and ejected the tape. Misty put it inside the case before she stretched out lazily on the couch and reached for the phone. She punched in the numbers on the dial pad and put the phone to her ear.

Thomas answered on the second ring. Misty smirked as she apologized for her abrupt departure. Her brother briefly scolded her and asked if she had spoken with their little sister lately. Misty told him it had been more than a week. Thomas suggested that they both should reach out to her, and Misty agreed.

"Thomas, do you miss us as kids sometimes. The way we used just to sit, talk, laugh, and stuff." Misty asked.

"Of course, I do. It's just life you know. I think about you two all the time. What is up with you now? I see you came alone, why is that Misty, you are a beautiful sister. You shouldn't be alone." Thomas said.

"You sound like a dad now; Thom cut it out."

"He's right. At this point, you could be hitched to a tree and we would take it. Nobody cares about your lifestyle anymore, and that is old news. I love you, and I want you to be happy."

"That's just it Thom; I made a date with an active man."

"Huh? Oh well, wait for a living man, is he a brother?"

"Yeah, faded, attractive, well-spoken, pants at the waistline and so on."

"Can we meet him?"

"If it turns out to be something, I'll let you know."

"Yeah, you do that!"

"Bye Thomas"

"Tell my new Bro I said what up doe!"

"Bye Thom"

"In a minute, Misty. What did dad say about that goodbye shit? Don't talk like that, it seems like goodbye means I'll never see you again."

"In a minute, love you."

"Love you too."

Misty hung up. She looked over at the Oak grandfather clock and noted it was nearly noon. Her vacation would be up soon. Misty wanted to make the best of the days she had left. It was only a few minutes past twelve when her phone rang again. She reached over and gripped the cradle to her ear.

"Hello?' Misty crooned.

"Hi Ms. Base, how is your day going?" a deep voice echoed.

"Fine, and to whom am I speaking with?"

"Kaiden, please Misty there's no need to be formal with me."

"Oh, Hi! How's your day going?"

"Better now. I was wondering what or where you wanted to eat later. Any ideas?"

"Whatever you want to eat, wherever you want to go, it's the first date so..."

Kaiden held the phone while a coughing spasm overtook him. Misty waited. After a few moments, Kaiden regained his composure. He struggled to hold in his laughter. Misty could feel his smile through the phone.

'Hello, are you there?' Misty asked at last.

"Yeah, for sure. I'm there, I meant I'm here," Kaiden answered.

"We'll figure it out later then okay. We can just ride around and decide if that's okay with you."

"I liked your first answer."

It was Misty's turn to hide her giggles. He had noticed her little play on words. She immediately decided that she liked his swag. Kaiden could flirt back without being ghetto.

"Do you want me to call you when you get off?" Misty asked.

"Is that how it works? You call me when I get off. That might be awhile so why don't you just call me when you get off instead?"

"Kaiden, I'm not at work, you called my house remember?"

"Yeah, but I still want you to call me when you get off. Don't worry if you need to call me several times, that works for me. I will be there at seven. See you soon Misty."

"Later, Kaiden."

Misty softly dropped the phone into the holder. Her dimpled cheeks beamed a glow. Something about Kaiden voice made Misty feel sensuous. She rolled off the couch and stood while she gazed at the receiver for a second longer.

She strolled into the kitchen and looked around. Her house was cute, but it had been a long time since she had entertained there. She thought about Kaiden once more. Misty decided to surprise him with a home-cooked meal.

She began to flutter effortlessly around her kitchen. She pulled out a copper-bottomed pan to sauté' some fresh asparagus. A cast iron skillet for New York Strip steaks and a baking sheet for herb crusted parmesan potatoes. Misty found a crystal bowl under the sink for a fresh Ceaser salad. She pulled down a bag of day old wheat rolls and laid them on the counter.

It took Misty longer to decide on dessert than dinner. Twenty minutes later, she had narrowed it down to either chocolate strawberries or hot fudge sundaes. She found a Bottle of Seagram's Platinum and Pinot Noir under the China cabinet and threw them both on the fridge's door. At last, she decided on the chocolate covered berries.

Misty leaned over the counter and placed her finger in her mouth. She nibbled nervously on the side of her nail. Kaiden seemed charming, seductive, and a little classy. He had most definitely shown that he could flirt and hold his own. Misty rolled her eyes up in her head and smiled. Naughty thoughts had crept into her mind before she willed herself to find an outfit for the night.

It had to be something sexy. Still, she had already decided against too hot. She wanted him to be attracted but not an invitation to have sex on the spot. She raced into her bedroom to find the thing to set the night off.

CHAPTER EIGHT

By four, an exotic blend of garlic and herbs had filled the house. Misty had found her outfit, washed her hands, and headed to the stove. She needed plenty of time to prepare properly and present the food. In the process, she located several votive candleholders. Misty placed them around strategically as the only light source they would have tonight.

It did not take long before Misty settled on a simple black dress with strapped stilettoes. The top of the dress showed her mocha colored cleavage well. A small slit ran midway her thigh while the slanted hem of the dress rested at her calves. Misty had a little extra padding in her tummy, but otherwise, she was firm. The dress accentuated her best curves.

At five precisely, the phone rang yet again. She had just seasoned the steaks and wrapped them in plastic for a quick marinade. She put the uncooked meat into the refrigerator, slammed the door, and hurried to answer the phone.

"Hello?" Misty said.

"Hi Misty, I hope I'm not coming across as a pest, but I was wondering if you would like for me just to pick up something and go back to my place or somewhere that we can talk. I would like to get to know, you know a chance to vibe with you without a bunch of people around." Kaiden blurted.

"No Kaiden, I won't go to your house. I'm glad you have your house, but I think it would be best if you just got dressed and came here at seven."

"Then that's what we will do. See you in a few hours."

"Okay"

Misty pushed the end call button. She frantically dialed Thomas's number. She listened as it rang several times before it went to voicemail. Misty ran her free hand through her hair. She slammed down the phone in frustration.

She had barely taken two steps to the kitchen before her line rang back. She pounced on the phone and sent the base skittering across the floor. By the time she put the receiver to her ear, the line had gone blank. Misty hit redial, and Thomas came through almost instantly.

"What's up Sis?" Thomas said.

"He called me twice; I'm in over my head. I cannot do this Thomas," Misty wailed.

"You can't do what Misty?"

"Have dinner with this guy."

"You don't like him like that or what? I don't understand."

"No, I like him. I don't know what to do with him, though. He is coming across as mature and responsible. I am out of my league here Thom. What would a person like that want to see me? I meant I don't think that. Meaning it is not as if I don't know to deal with a man. I don't even know what to say to a guy like that! This is going to be a disaster."

"Ummm yeah, pump the brakes. Talk a little about you, ask a little about him. Try to find common ground and just be yourself. You are lovable as it is. Shit, I'm shocked somebody hasn't scooped you up already anyway. Misty, are you nervous because it's a guy?"

"Exactly, plus I do not want to get to serious about anything. I planned to come home. "

"Well listen, if that's what you want, then I'd say go for it. It is a brother right?"

"Yes. Still, I don't know what I want. If anything at all. I have been single for so long that it is my comfort zone you know. You deal with people all the time. Your student's, their parents, volunteers, other teachers, even the party people at Nikki's. As for me, not so much. I don't know if I can hold a couple of hours of conversation with the opposite sex."

"You can and will do whatever you put your mind to, Misty. You always have."

"You're the success, Thom. You took every skill you had and did something spectacular. I wish Mom were here. I need to talk a woman right now. If…"

Thomas gasped in the phone. Misty put her hand over her mouth. Since their mother had passed, her sudden death had been a touchy subject. However, the loss was one that had been carried deeply by her children.

"You will not be ruled by fear. You are a Base. Let someone else whine about it." Thomas said.

"We go and try for it because if IF were a fifth, then we would all be drunk!" Misty chimed in.

"Exactly. That is what Ma would probably say. Look I have to get on to this gig at eight. I'll call you later and check on you, okay? Misty I wish that you would consider coming home. The children miss you, and we do too."

"I'll think about it. In a minute, Thom."

"In a minute, Sis."

Misty ended the call. After she had spoken with Thomas, she felt reassured. Misty had always been strong-willed, but Thomas's opinion mattered to her. He was one of the few people that she knew that could usually see both sides of an issue. He had been a steady voice of logic and reason to both of his sisters. After the phone call, Misty realized that she had a little more than an hour left to clean up and make her presentable. The race against time was on with a sprint into the kitchen.

CHAPTER NINE

Thomas sat at his desk and absent-mindedly tapped out a rhythm on the wood with his fingers. It was a habit, which he had developed as a child, whenever he was deep in thought. He had known about his sister's preference for many years. It was something that Misty didn't flaunt but certainly took no pains to hide. Now, his oldest sister had a date with not only a man, but also a brother.

Sometimes it annoyed Thomas that Misty had put him on a pedestal. Then there were times like this when he realized that she needed him. Thomas had things going on in his life. He was in the middle of a trial separation from his wife, had just moved into his place, and his teenage son Thomas Jr. had come to live with him. He often wondered about his daughter from a previous relationship. He felt the pains of life the same as those around him.

Even growing up, as kids, the differences between the three siblings were clear. Thomas was the kind of person that took lemons and made lemonade. Misty was the one that more likely to take it and throw it upside someone's head. While their baby sister, was more likely to eat the lemon.

Thomas stretched his legs out and rubbed his knee. Years of marching in any weather had begun to surface on his body. His natural size had also become a factor. Thomas had recently decided to lose a few pounds by changing his diet. I hope that that would help with the aches.

Then there were the women. Thomas believed in love and marriage, but since word got out of his separation, women were tripping over him. He was by most standards, a decent catch. Thomas had charm. Nevertheless, he had hopes of saving his marriage.

After months of discouraging interactions with his soon to be ex-wife, he met Classy. She was just as her name suggested. Classy was a tall, brown-skinned, woman with a pleasant personality, and flowing, jet-black hair. She had been patient and kind about his current position. She worked as the Director of Human Resources while she pursued a Master's degree in Human Development. She was a welcomed breath of fresh air in his life.

Thomas heard a stampede of footsteps. His office door burst open. A handful of his band members had come in and begun to talk excitedly. Thomas' fingers drummed faster.

"Mr. T, they bout to fight for real doe. The Hood Rats came up here and wanna battle our drum line toe to toe, but it be only be fourteen of us and fifteen of them." A student said.

Thomas got up and cracked his knuckles. He sighed heavily. Marching bands had the same dynamics as a sports team. His was sure his students were on fire about an immediate challenge on their home turf. He did not say a word as he stepped from behind his desk and followed his kids.

The crowd walked straight down the length of the main hallway to a set of double doors. He pushed the door handle with his massive hand, and it swung open with ease. Now, he could see the parking lot full of students. He closed the gap between him and the center of the gathering quickly.

"Where's Big Boy?" Thomas yelled.

"He went to get his drum key." someone replied from the crowd.

Thomas scanned the group of teenagers. He knew his players by face and name. Thomas immediately recognized the students that were not from his school. He strolled over to them and towered above them.

"Where ya drum major at?" He asked.

"Right here," a thin teenage boy said.

"Alright then my man, tell me what your name is then step on up and let's get this popping. What are the rules?"

"My name is Blink; they call me that cause I tap so sure, and quick that you hear me before you can see me. Y'all punked us at the Thanksgiving Parade cause we had players that were gone for the holiday vacation. We came to get what is rightfully ours. We want our props in a toe to toe. These wussies squawking cause they short one." Blink said.

"Chill with the name-calling. You're here squawking for the same reason. So you want a toe-to- toe, you got it. Somebody find Nicole and tell her that she is needed for a challenge."

Blink guffawed. He popped his polo shirt collar and put his hand over his mouth. The boy began to shake his head back and forth in disbelief. At last, he did not attempt to disguise his mocking laughter.

"What's so funny son? I want to laugh too." Thomas asked.

"Y'all got a chickenhead on yo team. This is going to be a cakewalk. Can't no female get down with us, but since we caught you slipping, use what you got. No disrespect." Blink said.

A plump soft-spoken girl emerged from the crowd with a snare drum strapped to her. Her face was blank as she stared at Blink. She reached into the side pocket of her khaki pants and retrieved a set of drumsticks. With her free hand, she adjusted the brim of her Detroit City baseball cap. Her other hand rested the sticks lightly on the skin of the drum.

Thomas moved back. Nicole walked up and stopped a few feet from a still smiling Blink. He looked around at his section members. They immediately formed a single line formation. Now, it was up to the Base team to step to whatever student they wished for the playoff. Thomas kept quiet as Big Boy hoisted his bass drum into position.

Thomas slid a hand into his pocket. He smirked. A faint hint of a smile registered across Nicole's face. Thomas reasoned at that moment that she had indeed heard her rivals' jeers. He gave a curt nod in her direction.

"Earn your respect. Break the wall down, 36 bars at a time!" Thomas said.

The opposing side started with the 'We built this City". One by one, each player beat out his part into a rock and roll styled finale. Thomas smiled and clapped. He shrugged and looked over at his students.

Nicole took one tiny step closer to the major on the other side. She relaxed her shoulders and lowered her eyelids. She took her sticks and twirled them flawlessly between her fingers before she hit the snare. With speed and agility, she played the first bars of "We will Rock you". At the end of their song, the entire drum line yelled, "You know."

Thomas's face had a strange glow about it as he listened intently, until the end. His students did not look to the other side. Instead, they looked to their director. Thomas rubbed his chin but gave no clue to as to his opinion.

Emboldened by Thomas's lack of response, Blink's section went into a recital of "This is how we do it." The heat glared down. The sun flickered bits of sparkle from the drums rim and the sweat on their respective players faces. Blink's team gave it their all. Their performance was close to musical perfection. Then Blink threw one of his sticks up in the air. When it came down, he failed to catch it.

Thomas's students remained quiet while Blink recovered his stick. Blink groaned at the mumbled insults from his teammates.

His eyes darted around nervously after he stood up. Still, Thomas's kids kept their composure.

After a lengthy awkward silence, Thomas' line gave an animated reply. One by one, in order of first to last they lifted their eyes to meet those of their challengers. They smiled. From the first note, the player's took steps forward, which cause the other side to have to take a step back. The air filled with the modified soul version delivery of "Who's House?"

Thomas laughed in spite of himself. In focused formation, his side had backed up Blink's line to the edge of the school threshold. Thomas ran his hand over his chest with a touch of pride. He walked down to the end of the lot to catch up with the students.

"Mr. T, who won this?' Someone asked from the crowd.

"I think we should ask Blink for his opinion since at the moment he's the representing director for his side right?" Thomas replied.

Blink's eyes darted up to meet Thomas's at the mention of his reference to him as the "director". Thomas raised his eyebrow at the boy. Blink straightened his previously defeated stance. He seemed to sense that Thomas had just raised the bar on his expectations.

Blink's mouth flipped opened and closed, like a fish out of the water. He swiveled his head around at those who had come to him and his surroundings. Once he centered his current position, gathered his wits, and braced his spine, he responded.

"I'ma give it to ya'll this time. I think we did magnificently but I messed up and ya'll stepped us back. So this time, it's a closer call ...but ya'll get it. This was extra practice for us though." Blink said.

The crowd, which were mostly students from Thomas's school cheered. They jumped and twirled in the air. Palms slapped and stung from a series of enthusiastic high-fives. Thomas let them enjoy it for a few moments before he shushed them.

"You're going to make an excellent Band Director soon, Blink. When you going to graduate?" Thomas asked.

"This my last year. Ima senior." Blink said.

"You applied for a school yet, check, and see if you can get a scholarship or something yet. If not, you need to get that squared away."

"Going to MSU with a 3.6 GPA to study Biotechnologies."

"You a science guy huh? All right then, gets it in. I hope to see you back here in a few years."

Blink nodded and turned to take the long walk back to where they had come from. Nicole cleared her throat, and Blink turned his head toward the sound. He rolled his eyes and flinched. His eyes widened when she balled up her fists.

"Dang, show some love," Nicole said.

Blink smiled. He balled his fist up too. He extended his fist forward and waited. He could not help himself and smiled brightly when Nicole gently bumped his fist with hers

CHAPTER TEN

Misty had managed to clean the kitchen, set the table, shower, and then tackled her mess of hair by 6:30. She had half an hour to apply a little color to her face and then slide into her outfit. She walked into her bedroom and started. She was ready a scant three minutes before 7:00.

The sun had already begun to fade away behind the mountains that shadowed the Valley, where she lived. She closed the blinds to block out any remaining light. Misty walked into the kitchen and opened a drawer near the sink. Silverware rattled as she pushed the tray back and forth in search of matches. Once she found them, she closed the drawer, opened the book, took on, and lit it. Misty slowly made her way to the living room and kitchen lighting the candles that she had set out earlier.

When she was done, she stood back and tried to gauge the mood of the room. It felt cozy to her. Not enough light to see in detail but just enough to see everything. She wanted Kaiden to be comfortable. Somehow, he had caused her to think romantically.

Misty was satisfied with the set as it were. She opened the closet door and grabbed her purse. It took a few tries but at last, she located what she wanted. Misty pulled out a bottle of a bottle of "Diamonds" perfume and uncapped it. She sprayed a few drops behind her ears, over her cleavage, and a spritz on her wrist. She returned the bottle to her bag and rubbed her wrists together.

The sound of footsteps on her porch startled her. She smoothed down her dress, wiped the creases of her lips, closed the closet, and put her hand on the knob of the front door. The light, sparkly scent hung delicately in the air around her. Misty turned the knob and opened the door.

Kaiden had his hand in the air poised to knock when the door swung open. He looked down into Misty's eyes and blushed. She lowered her eyelids and turned her head away from him while she gave him a quick hint of a smile. Kaiden opened the screen and stepped inside. Misty walked away from him. Kaiden closed the door and followed her.

Misty stopped short of the sofa and turned to face Kaiden. He was dressed casually in jeans, and a button-up, with a blazer. His hair was neatly faded in a way that complimented his face. His hair was crisply tapered while a gold chain with a cross hung from his neck. Misty was pleased with his overall appearance.

He took a step towards her and extended his arms to embrace her. A sexy fragrance radiated from his body. Misty inhaled and stepped closer to Kaiden. She felt magnetically drawn into his waiting arms.

Kaiden cautiously circled his arms around her waist. He laced his fingers together in the small of her back above her plump hump. Misty grasped the hem of his jacket and laid her head on his chest. Maybe it was animal instinct, but they both broke away now that they realized that others scent had allured them. Kaiden cleared his throat and stepped back.

"You look beautiful, Misty. Where would you like to go?" Kaiden asked.

"You do too Kaiden. I was hoping that you did not mind staying in with me tonight. I made dinner for us. It's quiet, and I thought we'd be able to talk more freely at my house than a restaurant." Misty said.

"You stole my idea. Actually though, you can cook. What's on the menu?"

"New York Strip Steaks, Fresh Asparagus, and Roasted Potatoes with a Ceaser Salad."

"Sounds like a winner. Would you like for me to go out and grab drinks, some wine maybe?"

"No thank you, I have that covered in the fridge to chill. I have some Seagram's Platinum and lime juice if you dare to. I could use one right now."

Kaiden smirked while Misty turned and made her way to the kitchen. His nostrils flared as he watched looked her over from behind. There was a slight jiggle in her hips as they swayed. Her smooth skin flashed him through the slit her dress. Kaiden was glad he had come.

Misty opened the China cabinet and took out two rock glasses. She walked them over to the sink, cut on the water, and rinsed them. Kaiden ventured into the kitchen to offer assistance. Misty had not heard him come in and turned right into his well-defined chest while going to the fridge. She put her small, delicate fingers on his chest and her index rested on his a portion of his exposed skin.

Her heart thumped wildly in her chest. He felt and smelled amazing to her. Misty resisted the urge to wrap her arms around his neck by standing still. Kaiden did not speak until Misty looked up at him.

"I'm sorry if I startled you, I came to see if I could help with anything."

Misty felt her body tense with expectation. With her hand a mere few inches from his muscular neck, she sighed. Her breasts firmly pressed into his chest. Only fabric prevented skin-to-skin contact. That did little to quell the intense chemistry that had begun to boil between the two. Kaiden's eyes searched Misty's face for an answer. While Misty thoughts whispered a seductive drawl that she could not relay to Kaiden.

(Yes Kaiden. You can help me with a taste of those soft lips. You can help by knocking everything off this counter, putting me on the edge, and taking full advantage of this moment. Please do not kiss me; this thong is not equipped to hold back the results from that.)

"Not right now." Misty murmured.

She thought her reply would be enough for Kaiden to move. She needed him just to step back a little. The physical closeness of his body was driving her insane. Kaiden remained right where he was.

Her eyes were dark as night. The throaty tone of her voice sent shivers down his back. Her perfume along with her hand on his chest had scrambled his senses, shortly. Kaiden heard her, but his body did not want to move thus far. He swallowed hard and gazed into the windows of her soul.

Misty turned her head and broke away. She shimmied herself from in between Kaiden and the counter. Misty walked over to the fridge, opened the door, and took out the Vodka and juice. Kaiden had picked up the glasses and held them out for her to fill. She sat the juice bottle on the counter, unscrewed the cap from the liquor, and poured a double shot in each glass. When she was done, she traded bottles to add a splash of juice.

Kaiden lifted a cup of the bright green concoctions to his lips. He sipped and grimaced. Misty giggled and took the other glass from him. She pivoted and strolled into the living room with her drink. Misty left Kaiden to balance his drink, according to his taste.

Less than a minute had passed when he joined Misty on the couch. A portion of her dress had fallen between her thighs. Her silky skin glowed with a delicate sheen, from her exposed thigh on down. Neatly trimmed and polished toes lay comfortable in her shoes. He had noticed that she presented herself well.

To get another whiff of her perfume, Kaiden sat close. Their outer thighs touched. Kaiden was relieved that the candlelight was bright enough for him to get a good look at all of her. Now that she had sat down, her dress strained to cover her breasts. The urge to rest his face in the gorge of them was terrible. In place of that, he inhaled before he sipped his drink.

Kaiden sat his glass on the coffee table and turned to Misty. He took a finger and brushed a wayward strand of hair that had fallen near her eye away. Misty had the glass up to her lips. She quickly pour a little of the fruity mix into her mouth, swished and swallowed. When Kaiden' hand touched hers to take the glass from her mouth, Misty stifled a moan.

Kaiden took the glass and softly placed it on the table with a clink. He turned his attention back to Misty and leaned in closed to her face. She ran her tongue over one side of her bottom lip and bit down on it. Except for the hum of appliances and their breaths, the house was quiet.

Darkness had settled in. In the distance thunder roared from an approaching storm. Tension hung in the air between the two of them. Although the living room was mostly a large open space, it seemed intimate and small.

"Tell me Misty, what are you thinking about?" Kaiden asked.

His mouth was only a few inches from her full, glossy lips. As he pronounced each word, smooth warmth came from him. Misty could feel the breeze-like heat fan at the base of her throat. It traveled down to the hills of her breasts and dissipated. This was the third time that he had been close enough to taste.

Misty reached up and smoothly arranged her hand on his neck. Contact with his skin sent a jolt of sizzling current to her most intimate parts. Kaiden leaned even closer and stopped less than an inch from her lips. Misty barely parted her lips, before she left no distance between them at all.

CHAPTER ELEVEN

Thomas had dispersed the students after the impromptu battle for musical respect. Both sides had encouraged each other. They agreed to continue their efforts at the Michigan State Fair Parade. Thomas pulled Blink to the side, and shook his hand before he left him with his parting words.

"Blink, whatever happens in life, don't stop the music. I see greatness in you." Thomas said.

The young man shook his hand and blushed. Thomas watched for a brief second when the crowd crossed the street. He then went back to the school. A hyped rally of his students followed behind him. The kids chattered nonstop until Thomas blew the whistle that hung around his neck.

"This ain't the choir. We can sing together but we can't all talk, at the same time." Thomas said.

Nicole came up to him and stood next to him. He reached out and gave her a congratulatory hug. She radiated. Nicole looked up at her Band Director.

"Are there any more objections today about having a female on the line with us?" Thomas asked.

BIG BODY BASE II

The fellows looked at each. No one objected. Nicole had stepped and played her part without a mistake. Her presence out on the parking lot had not only made the battle a true toe-to-toe, but her presence had also made the other team a little cocky. The result of which was the majors' attempt to show off and swung a tight race in their favor.

"Good. I do not expect to hear anything else about who can do what around. She is my sister, but that is not why she is here. She here' because she good on those drums. Look around you; remember your humbled beginnings. Do not block somebody from a chance because they do not fit your image of a role. Give them a chance because they deserve it. I was very proud of every single one of you out there today. You did not just show your skills; you showed class. Now, get out of my office. It's time for me to lock up and go home." Thomas said.

A few more students walked up and hugged him. A few shook his hand. The rest either nodded his way or gave him daps on the way out. He hung around until the last student, Nicole, remained.

"Let me guess, you need a ride home?" Thomas asked.

Nicole nodded yes and sniffed. He sighed heavily. Since their mother had passed, their father had fallen into a trance-like state. Nicole had relied on Thomas for moral and sometimes financial support.

Misty moved out of the state shortly afterward, unable to bear the constant reminders of her mother. Her children had begun to

60

act out. The simple schoolyard fights had turned into violent street brawls. In addition to the true evil that Judas brought into her life, she saw her children circling the drain of big city life.

One day, after arriving home from work she encountered a mass of children fighting in front of her house. She had barely parked her White Windstar before she leaped out. She quickly snatched her three children, nephew, and little sister from the melee'. Misty sent the other kids involved in brawl away.

Exhausted from a long day at the office, she dragged herself into the house too. She took one look at the five scratched and sweaty bodies that lay in various positions on the couch, chair, and floor. It was a Thursday. The fourth time that week that she'd come home to find her children had been involved in something short of a gang war. She did not ask what happened, this time. Instead, she went up to her bedroom and made reservations for two hotel rooms in the country for a week.

Misty had already decided the day before. She would quit her job, move to cow country or for that matter to the moon, to save her children. She did not intend to bury a child of hers or from her community over street violence. The next morning, she got up to a busted window in her van. It solidified her resolve to move them away.

In the flurry of the next two weeks, Misty had found a house, quit her job, and packed an 18 wheel U-Haul with her truck in tow.

She left behind everything she knew. She hoped that a change of environment would be good for the kids.

Thomas had thrown himself into his work with a newfound fervor. His mother's death had left an inexplicable void in his life. One minute everything in their lives was based on their mothers' wishes and advice. The next minute none of them could even call her. She never saw her fiftieth birthday. Thomas leaned on music to carry him through one of the toughest times in life.

His mother was very young when she had given birth to him, at fifteen years old. While she cared for Thomas in the role of a parent, their age difference also lent a big sister-like place in his life. The loss for him was a double whammy. He was her only son.

The calls between the two oldest siblings had become much less regular. Thomas had not received a phone call before Misty's departure. She called him almost a month later and told him. She promised to return to see him soon.

Thomas walked to the last door. He draped his arm around his little sisters' shoulder. He took one last look around and shut off the lights. Thomas was unusually quiet. Once in the lot, Thomas retrieved his keys, unlocked the doors, and started the car. Nicole got in and slammed the door.

He did not say anything on the drive to the house. When he pulled up, he looked over at Nicole. Tears ran down her cheeks. Thomas put the car in drive and pulled off. He realized that at times it was too hard for her to step foot into the house. He father had remained in the house where the memories of his wife were most evident. For a barely legal teenager, though it was not comforting. Thomas saw the look on her face and took her home with him.

Thomas pulled up to McDonalds and gave her a twenty from his visor to get food. When she came back and passed him a Coke, he said thanks and took off. Half an hour later, they were at his house. After he had parked, the siblings went inside.

Nicole went straight for the shower while Thomas sat on his leather sofa. His home had been tastefully decorated and fully furnished. He leaned over and picked up the receiver of his cordless phone. He called their father. No one answered at first.

Finally, his dads' voice came on the line. Thomas told him that the baby girl was with him. He would bring Nicole home sometime later in the week. Then he asked his father how he was.

The men talked for a brief time. The strain to avoid the mention of his deceased wife was evident in the crackling of his voice. There was a constant, unspoken grief. Each member of the family tried their best to shoulder their share. It had become the routine without effort. Thomas ended his call with his father.

He leaned his head back and closed his eyes. On top of everything else, the Statewide Battle of the Bands was only a few weeks away. His band had earned their chance at the State Trophy and bragging rights. Thomas had received the notice a month ago.

He immediately informed the students. He promised that if they continued to do their best, he would help them. That same evening, he stayed late to put in the request for field trip permission and transportation. Thomas would have to wait almost two weeks for an answer from the school board.

Detroit Public School had sent him a memo that morning. The board had granted permission to take the children up to Lansing, Michigan with a parent's signature. However, the funds needed for the buses were denied. The system did not have it to spare.

For Thomas, it was bittersweet news. He could take them, but Thomas had to figure out how to get all of them there and home, with approved transportation. It would be an out-of-pocket expense. That was not possible on a Band Director's salary.

Detroit Public Schools could barely afford books. Many teachers already sat aside part of their pay to purchase needed items. Essentials such as toilet paper, Composition books, pencils, hand sanitizer and so on. Most of them showed up to work daily, simply for the love of teaching alone.

Thomas accepted that his plate of life was full. Still, he could not rest. He had given his kids his word. He sighed again.

"With great talent comes great responsibility," Thomas said to him.

The student would be there to compete. He did not have a solid plan as of yet. Thomas worked different angles in his mind. He fell asleep from exhaustion, His last conscious thought was wherever there is a will, and then there is a way.

Two hours later, he awoke with a start. He got up from the couch and rubbed the tight muscles in his neck. He shook the cobwebs from his head. Thomas picked up the phone in the wee hours of the morn. A plan had formed in his sleep.

The phone beeped as Thomas located his caller ID roster. He scrolled through the numbers. He counted more than a dozen calls he could make once daylight broke. Organizations called on him all the time. He hoped that he could find a few that would allow the children to have a car-wash fundraiser on their site.

A somewhat relieved Thomas returned the phone to its holder. He could only get a few more hours of rest before it was time to go again. Thomas pulled off his shoes and coerced his limbs to work with him on the way to shower. Twenty minutes later, a fresher Thomas exited the bathroom in pajamas. He walked down the hall to his room. Nicole lay peacefully asleep in the middle of his bed. Thomas pulled the door up, walked back down the hall, and promptly stretched out of the couch.

He fidgeted around for a moment. Soon, Thomas was still. A nasal snore came from the couch. Thomas had drifted back off to sleep, without dinner.

CHAPTER TWELVE

Kaiden's' lips tasted like sweet cream to Misty. She sucked and nibbled at them for a moment. Finally, Kaiden' tongue parted her pillow lips, in search of hers. He took a hand and glided it over her naked thigh. Misty whined tenderly. The flavor of him had already embedded itself in her brain.

Misty melted while she slithered backward. Rational thought escaped her as Kaiden's' hand travel closer to her pot of honey. Kaiden exhaled. Misty drank his tongue deep inside of her after he did.

Misty closed her thighs abruptly. She struggled to contain the force that amplified between her legs, from his kiss. Her womanhood surged snugly against the flimsy material of her thong. Now, Kaiden's' fingers burrowed between her solid legs.

Kaiden kissed a moist path down to the banks of her breast. Misty fingers crept down the last part of his head. He licked the cleft of her breasts. When Kaiden began to nibble at her flesh, Misty heard the raindrops pelt like applause on the windows of the house.

The wind howled. Candlelight flickered through the home. Kaiden pulled her dress out his way with his teeth. Her bare breasts wiggled out. Kaiden readily sucked it.

Misty sobbed aloud at the feeling of his mouth. Kaiden continued to bring Mist taunted pleasure with his lips. A tiny puddle of dew formed between legs. She wanted to taste Kaiden lips again. She coveted just another taste of his lips.

Misty tugged at Kaiden's' jacket. He interrupted his game of cat and mouse with her nipple. He looked up at Misty. A fiery hotness sent triggers from her eyes through him. He sat up to compose him.

:"What's wrong?" Kaiden whispered.

"We just met, Kaiden. I can't." Misty said.

"We're adults Misty. What is wrong? You're not feeling this?"

Misty chewed the inside of her mouth. She had little choice, but to eat the words that raged in her contemplations. The undisputable evidence that trickled from her body was a giveaway to her. No matter what came out her mouth, Kaiden had turned up the heat.

("Of course, I'm feeling you. I am so wet for you. I could slide down on you like an oily stripper pole. Hell, I know we're both grown. What is wrong is that I know that we just met, but every inch of me wants you. I want you to take me right here. Let's do things so thoroughly freaky, that I'll remember you when I get dementia. Take this and brand your name in my subconscious for the rest of my life. Feast on my energy while you channel the mysterious life force from deep into the heart. Stay the night; wake up in my house, and in my bed. Lose me in your storm, all night long. Make love to me, Kaiden)

"Kaiden, I'm attracted to you. It is just really too soon. I did not agree to this date to get laid. Would you like to help me finish dinner? I'm hungry." Misty stated.

Kaiden's eyes tracked her movements while she stood, rearranged her dress, and sauntered into the kitchen. He repositioned him on the sofa. A few more minutes and Kaiden would have unzipped and been surrounded by her walls. He smirked. She wanted to wait, and he could respect that.

"Yes, I just thought it was time to eat something." Kaiden said.

Misty paused. She threw a haughty look over her shoulder at him. Then Misty put a finger to her lip and caressed it. The warmth of his kiss was still there.

"You can't have any dessert if you're going to misbehave." Misty mocked.

"If I act up, will you send me to your bed without dinner too?" Kaiden quipped.

"Why you got to say it like that? Are you ready to have dinner or not Kaiden?"

Kaiden walked up to Misty. He wrapped his arms around her from behind. His hands conscientiously journeyed up the swells of her breasts. Misty bottom lodged firmly against his swollen manhood. Kaiden leaned into her right ear.

"I do believe that I was enjoying a rather tasty appetizer before you abruptly took it away." Kaiden murmured.

"Oh God, Kaiden please, it's been so long," Misty said.

"Two years is a long time. I understand, but it doesn't have to be that way."

Misty reached up, laid her hands on top of his, pulled away, and turned to face him. She looked up into his eyes. A radiant glow of a mature, gentle soul stared back. The urge, to be honest, overwhelmed her.

"Kaiden, it's been two years since I've had a lover. It's been closer to twenty years since it was with a man." Misty said.

CHAPTER THIRTEEN

Thomas woke up to the lovely sounds of birds chirps. The Detroit morning sun held the promise of a new day. As was his routine, he quickly got him ready for work. He took a moment to send up a prayer. He began to make a series of phone calls, to those that had reached out to him.

He was on the phone when his sister emerged from the bathroom ready for another at school. She had overheard a portion of his conversation. Her nose crinkled. Thomas hung up on the phone, called for her, and they left.

Once they arrived at the school, Thomas let her out to catch up with her classmates. Nicole had waved before she ran off into the crowd. Thomas parked in the teachers' lot and shut off the car. He rested his head on the steering wheel for a moment.

The phone calls hadn't gone as he had hoped. There were a few good leads, but he did not have solid dates yet. Time was a serious factor. He was determined that he would not stand in front of his band and tell them that they could not go to the State Finals. Something had to give and soon.

Thomas got out of the car, held his head up, and leisurely strolled into the building. His students would not know the worries he had. He knew that life would bring them many disappointments, as it were. He just preferred to keep them at a minimal on his watch.

As he walked up the hall filled with kids, he could hear bits and pieces of the lives of his students daily. He already knew the about the pain and suffering some of them went through every day. More than a handful of them had come to school just to be able to eat for the day. It was a great public shame that the children waded through.

He had seen it up close. It was the ugliest sight a man could imagine. The lost look of absolute physical hunger was pure horror. Even so, it was only of the many pangs of hunger that he saw in the halls and rooms.

Thomas often saw the desire for knowledge. It was that tiny ray of hope, which could steer the kids away from a tragic potentially tragic end. Most of his classes had with children raised by single mothers that worked hard to help their children. Thomas showed up to do his part.

His way happened to be with music. He did not just teach notes. More often than not, he shared with them the history, struggles, and triumphs of sound. He taught them to indulge life itself, even its harshness, with the joy of harmony.

Thomas was never one to take credit for anything that he accomplished. He regularly referred to the teachers that he worked with as teammates. If a student was not doing well in other subjects, he rode them to bring those grades up. He had no qualms about banning them from completion, if they did not, thus he became for many of them, a father figure too.

Thomas walked into the room. He saw Mrs. Yielder from the Math Department had waited for him. He waved her into his office and shut the door. Thomas could tell it was serious.

"Good morning, Mrs. Yielder. What can I do for you?" Thomas asked.

"I got two of yours that isn't going graduate, Mr. Base." Mrs. Yielder replied.

"Not a chance?"

"Unless they pass the final exam with an A, none. So far, their grades do not support it. A high mark on the final will push them just past a failing grade. I will be having lunch in my room if they need to find me. I will do whatever I can to help them, but they have to show me that they know this stuff. I have to be able to sleep at night."

"What seems to be the problem?"

"They skip my class Thomas, and the kicker is neither one of them are dummies. They just do not show up. I stay to tutor them. Hell, my daughter comes to help me tutor them. I cannot pass them if they do not know it. If I send these kids to the next level like this, then I become part of the problem. I understand the problem, which is not my team. I am not about to play any role in this "our kids don't stand a chance" bullshit either. They are not about to leave high school and cannot even pass Algebra I. They skip here and pass, they are not going to prepared to compete in the real world."

"Give me the names."

"Here they are."

Thomas took the sticky note offered by his teammates. His jawline tightened. He rolled his eyes up in frustration. At last, Thomas put his hand on his temple and rubbed it. He nodded his understanding at Mrs. Yielder, who promptly left to attend her class.

It was barely 8 a.m. Thomas sighed heavily. It was two of his best band members. He secretly wished that Corporal punishment were allowable for about two minutes. He'd readily split the time between the two of them.

Instead, he got up and went to teach his class. Once he walked out of the office and into the main portion of the huge Band Room, he paused. The room overflowed with students jammed wall to wall. He only expected his usual overcrowding of 49 bodies.

"What are yall doing?" Thomas asked.

"We were staging one of them protest thangs, Mr. T. They gone give us buses or we gone skip class until they do!" Someone yelled.

"You gone what? No, you're going to go to class, learn, and be here when the buses arrive to go State." Thomas said.

"I told them about the money problem for the buses, Mr. T," Nicole said.

"Oh, I'm sorry. I didn't know that you were the Band Director. I can do the math, from what I just heard from Mrs. Yielder some of us are caught in the struggle of putting their ass in a non-moving chair, five days a week. Seeing as how I know that those students come to school every day, even if I have to drive them here, so I do not understand how they could miss that class. That is something that will get them thrown out of the first chair in the drum line. In fact, that will get them thrown out the band. Now protest yourselves to class, now." Thomas said.

"I just thought…"

"That you can do better in Math? I know you can. You are banned from practice and State unless you pass that Final. If you can show up for practice, then you can stay for tutoring. What is wrong with yall? When you become famous musicians, you might want to be able to count the money. Get out of my room and get where you belong!"

The children were scattered. The talk of a sit-in was a lost memory as they headed for the safety of their respective classes. The sound of stampeding feet echoed in the halls. He waited until only silence remained.

"Take out your books and turn to page 12. We are going to play "How Great" to warm up." Thomas said.

A few squawks blasted in the air. They children giggled at the out of tune clarinet player. Thomas looked over at the offending player. The student snickered as she looked around the room. Thomas burst out with laughter too.

The stresses of life rolled away for a moment while Thomas gladly collected his pay. That was the highlight of many teachers life. The moment when they realized their students wanted to rise to levels of greatness. They were eager, ready to take a chance, willing to learn from their mistakes, and able to rise above anything.

For the dedicated, that look was why they did. The moment that to purchase supplies, lunch at their desks, parent-teacher conferences, and late nights to grade papers amidst of the usual insanity of life, paid off in full. The times when they saw seeds that they hoped to grow, take life.

The rest of the day's classes went without incident. By last the period, Thomas was exhausted. He decided to go down to Mrs. Yielder to make sure his kids had shown up, on the way out. He locked up the classroom and left.

He made his way down the corridor. It was only a matter of seconds before he could peek through the door of Mrs. Yielders' class. Thomas shook his head. He saw students crammed into her class. Some sat on the floor. Thomas smirked.

He had known Mrs. Yielder all of his life. She had a way with children too. From the amount bodies in her tutor session, one could only assume that he was not the only stop of the day. Mrs. Yielder would call on teachers, and then parents, then grandparents, neighbors, emergency numbers, whatever help she could get. Much like Thomas, the buck stopped at failure, just not on her watch.

Thomas took the journey to the car lot with a smile. The sun was still high in the sky. The great outdoors buzzed with traffic and the sounds of big city life. It had turned to be a decent day for him after all.

He had a while before his sister would be done with her studies. With the free time on his hands, he could either catch some sleep in the car or see Classy. He quickened his pace. He would much rather spend time in the presence of a beautiful woman.

CHAPTER FOURTEEN

Misty waited for Kaiden's reaction. She peered into his eyes. Her breath caught in her the throat. She saw a sensual hunger that she fully understood.

He rubbed his hand up the small of her back. Misty felt her body shiver. When she cast a glance towards the floor, Kaiden lifted her chin. She let out a deep sigh as Kaiden's' lip touched hers again.

"Did you hear me Kaiden?" Misty murmured.

"Mmmm hmmm." Kaiden breathed.

Kaiden pecked gently at her lips. He bent down and kissed the side of her neck. Her body tensed. Kaiden swept her into his arms.

Misty did not protest as Kaiden led her to the sofa again. He patted the empty spot next to him. She brushed some strands of hair out of the way so that she could see better. Her hair fell around her shoulders when she sat. She shook her head and stroked her hair into place.

"Misty, I don't care. I did not think that you were the one to have a bunch of lovers. Maybe, I'm the man to win your heart." Kaiden said.

"Win my heart? Kaiden we just met." Misty said.

"Yeah, so we get to know each other."

"You don't care."

"That you haven't made love to a man in years? Forgive me the way I'm about to say this, but that's a turn on."

"It is?"

"I'd like to have dinner now."

Kaiden watched from the couch. He could see her hips wiggle as she made her back in the kitchen. He paused and then leaned back on the sofa.

"Maybe, she thinks I'm playing with her." Kaiden thought.

It was only a short time before Misty returned to the front room with two plates of food. She sat a plate in front of him. Misty made another trip to get utensils and condiments. When she returned, Misty sat close to Kaiden. She looked over at Kaiden's' face. The glow of the candles made him look incredibly sexy to her.

Kaiden had not attempted to touch his food. Misty stayed quiet. She was not hungry for food. Misty wanted just another taste of Kaiden's' luscious lips again.

Three minutes passed, and neither one of them had lifted a fork. The awkward silence had stifled them. Misty took the quiet moment in peacefully. Kaiden seemed to be lost in his thoughts and his glare focused on nothing in particular.

At last, Misty decided to cover their plates and put them away for a while. Kaiden remained quiet while she did. She refilled their drinks, and turned on the radio, on the way to the couch. She sat very close to him.

"Kiss me damn you. You are just going to sit there and smell delicious. I mean you are a few minutes away from the best ride of your life. Do something. I do not want to make the first move. You already did it three times tonight, and I stopped yo..." Misty thought to her.

Misty put the drinks on the table. She crawled up into Kaiden's' lap. Misty put her hands on his chest and traced the outline of his muscular body up to his neck with both hands. Misty let her hands rest on his back. She pulled him to her and kissed him.

Kaiden ran his hand along her side He returned her kiss with passion. Misty could feel his maleness swell under her. The simple kisses, between them earlier, did not compare to this moment. Kaiden could feel her unreserved energy in her comeback.

"It seems that I hastily took away your appetizers. Then I took your dinner back for later. The only course left to have is dessert." Misty moaned.

"Mmmm hmmm." Kaiden said.

Misty stood up. She grabbed Kaiden's' hand. When he stood up, Misty led him from the couch and to her bedroom door. She stopped abruptly. Misty turned and wrapped her arms around Kaiden's' waistline.

"I have protection in case you don't have any," Misty said.

"You can still make babies?" Kaiden asked.

"Yes, and for personal protection too. Can you still make babies, Kaiden?"

"Yeah, I can."

"Okay, look I want to go in there. Serve you some umm dessert. If you're magnificent, you just might get another helping of dessert."

"The last one messed up dessert for twenty years. If I'm about to get dessert, then I'm not only prepared, protected, and ready but I you might as well be prepared to get me another helping."

Misty laughed at his charmed filled wit. She imagined he could be quite romantic, and maybe even, a poet at times. Once he ran his hand over her thigh again, Misty felt the sizzle in countless places. She opened her bedroom door and walked in with Kaiden in tow.

"Welcome to my home, Kaiden. This is my room. I sleep alone, in whatever I can find if anything at all. There is a bathroom right outside the door. If you'll excuse me for a moment, I'd like to go there and slide into something a little more comfortable." Misty said.

"Are you sure that you want to do this. I mean, we don't have to. I like your company without everything else, not to discourage you, though." Kaiden replied.

Misty strolled over to a seated Kaiden. She pulled the string that held her dress. It fell to the floor. Her black Victoria's Secret panty set hugged every curve. A new whiff of her "Diamonds" perfume floated up to his nostrils.

As her dress lay in a heap at her feet, Misty leaned over Kaiden and brought her breasts within an inch of his face. Her hair swung to one side while she picked her dress up from the floor.

Misty stood up and walked away to lay her dress across a chair near her window. Kaiden gulped. Misty sashayed out of the room. Dressed in only panties, a bra, and stilettoes, Kaiden carefully watched until she was no longer in view.

Misty paused in the doorway of her bathroom. She wondered if her actions had been too bold. A moment of uncertainty entered her mind. Then she distinctly heard the sound of a zipper come down.

CHAPTER FIFTEEN

Thomas had managed to locate some flowers on the way to see Classy, from a roadside vendor. She was about to leave her job for the day at Bright Technologies. He pulled up and presented her with the impromptu gift. Classy smiled. Thomas asked her to ride with him,

Classy happily obliged him. Thomas took her for a quick drive around the city. He asked how her day was. Thomas listened while she told him about her day.

Half an hour later, he returned her to her vehicle. He gave her a chaste kiss on the cheek and saw her to her car. Once she was safely in her car, he drove off. Thomas had to pick up his sister from her tutor session.

When he arrived back at the school, Nicole was waiting in the lot. She ran up to the car and got in. Thomas asked her how her day was. His sister passed him a note that had been stapled closed.

He opened it. Thomas frowned while he read. He folded the note and put it in his shirt breast pocket. Thomas pulled off.

"What it say, Thom?" Nicole asked.

"I'm going to wait until you pass the exam, and then I'll show it to you. You are going to pass the exam right. Do you need me, to set up some additional tutoring, or do you think that Mrs. Yielder can teach you this? Thomas asked.

"I understood her today."

"Okay, what are we having for dinner?"

"I don't care."

"Yeah, guess I need to see your English teacher too huh?"

Nicole laughed. Thomas laughed with her. He reached over and patted the back of her hand. He was pleased with the note.

Thomas pulled up in front of the Outback Steakhouse. His sister squealed with delight. He had barely parked before she leaped from the car. He had decided to have a decent sit-down dinner for a change of pace.

After supper, Thomas drove back to the apartment. Once his sister settled in, he went to turn on his large screen television. Thomas had barely relaxed when the phone rang. Thomas groaned.

"Even my time off doesn't fell like my time off?" Thomas mumbled.

He answered the phone. Thomas listed to the animated callers' voice. He rubbed his chin. A soft glow creased his cheeks.

When Thomas hung up the phone, he instantly relaxed. The Butzel Center had agreed to let the children come and wash cars. It was one of the few community centers open. Mrs. Yielder would be able to help with flyers, he hoped.

With a few weeks left, this took some of the pressure from the situation. The evening news was on. It only took a few moments of peace. Thomas drifted out into a restful slumber.

It was late at night when Thomas woke. He looked at his caller ID. He had several missed calls. Thomas felt rested but did not hear the phone.

Thomas managed to move his tired body to the shower. He bathed and slipped into his nightclothes. When he returned to the sofa, Nicole sat there.

"What's wrong?" Thomas asked.

"Nothing, I heard you were up?" Nicole replied.

"Get your rest baby, I'm okay, I just wanted to shower."

"Okay"

Thomas watched as his sister padded down the hall. The couch was not the most comfortable place, but he just felt like he needed to keep her with him. It was only a temporary situation. Sometimes a change of scenery did him good. He wished the same for her, now.

The next morning, Thomas had to leave earlier than usual. He had to attend a staff meeting for the heads of Departments. This was his chance to present his concerns about the lack of funding directed to the needs of the children. Thomas put on his good church clothes.

Once he was dressed, he gave himself the once over in the mirror. He was happy with what he saw. Despite the trials and tribulations of life, he was ready. Thomas had thought long and hard about what he wanted to say. He had to get the authorities to understand.

Thomas had not gotten lost in his position of power. He had come from the streets. He had lost loved ones to violence, suicide, drugs, and drink. He had seen the faces of the student who did not make it. He had made phone calls to reach out to relatives of children that were in trouble. Always hoping that something positive intervened for the children.

Thomas had been to many funerals. He had seen it all from the destructive to the self-destructive. It seemed to be a never-ending battle, at times. Then it there was days such as this. His turn to present the realities of the children's lives in front of the decision makers.

They needed to see the struggle. To understand that while some went home to a cozy home, had dinner slept in a bed, or who were drove there in a car. That the children did not always have those things. They needed Fine Arts, World History, and resources. Committees based on reports cut programs to make way for fancier things. Thomas saw the need, for basics such as transportation for trips, books, instruments, more teachers, and healthier food, for students citywide.

He had a surprise for their guests today. He had chosen a few students to speak on their homes lives. He wanted them to hear first-hand what the kids went through. He picked student that came to school regularly, but had serious challenges. One student walked over two miles there and back everyday.

The same student often fought because he was picked on. His shoes were in terrible condition. More often than not, he was there in time for breakfast at 7:30 am. He arrived clean, but he had not had a haircut in months.

Had it not been for some of the business leaders in the community, the schools would have collapsed a long time ago. The city of Detroit was aware of their problems. They rallied around their children, their future, and rolled up their sleeves. It was their house and future at stake too.

Thomas was unaware, but there would be a surprise waiting for him, as well. He waited until his sister was ready. Thomas and his sister locked up and went to the car. He had an unusual feeling in his gut. It was not doom, but he could feel something. He dismissed the instinct and left for work.

Thomas pulled up to the teachers' lot. He scratched his head. The lot was crowded with students and staff. Thomas parked and looked over at Nicole. She hid her smile and looked out the window. Thomas heard someone scream. He jumped from the car and raced towards the sound.

CHAPTER SIXTEEN

Misty felt a chilly breeze wisp over her nearly naked body. She pinned her hair up in a loose bun. She cut on the water and refreshed her. As a last minute thought, Misty touched up her lip-gloss and added a fresh touch of "Diamonds" to her essential areas.

Her heart fluttered wildly in her chest. She had been extremely disappointed in the past. She could not believe that she was about to go there again. There was something different about Kaiden though.

Misty took a deep breath. Kaiden awaited her presence. The potential for love was on the other side of the wall. All she had to do was walk into the room.

Kaiden looked up when Misty came into the room. He swallowed hard again. Kaiden got up and walked up to Misty. He bent down and kissed her.

Misty wrapped her arms around him. Kaiden pulled her closer. Hungrily his lips traveled over her flesh. Her body came alive under his caressing kisses.

Misty did not protest when Kaiden lead her to the bed. He had not undressed. Kaiden waited while Misty sat lengthwise on the mattress. He stepped back.

His eyes took in every inch of her sculpted body. The way she glided in heels had gotten his undivided attention. Misty noticed that Kaiden eyes were on her feet. She reached down to take off her shoes, but he stopped her.

"If you don't mind, I'd like you to leave those on," Kaiden whispered.

The words to reply never came to her lips. The room seemed warm to her. She brought her hand up to cover her mouth while Kaiden took off his shirt. A few seconds later, his pants were off too.

Misty tried to conceal her thoughts. Even in the dimly lit room, Misty could see that he was well equipped. His satiny boxers' shorts strained to capacity in the front. Misty did her best not to let the awe show on her face.

Kaiden eased closer to Misty. He reached down and unsnapped her brassiere from its front latch. The material fell away. Her exposed breasts jutted in the air in defiance of gravity. Meanwhile, Kaiden looked on.

Kaiden kneeled on the side of the bed. He started a path of kisses from in between the cleft of her firm melons. Misty bit her lip. Finally, he touched her soft inner thigh with his lips.

When Kaiden pulled the band of her panties to the side, Misty flinched. Then he cleverly looped her panties around his protruding thumb. Misty scooted up. Kaiden did not have to search for his dessert. It peeked out from her a little. He saw the firmness of her desire as it glistening with sweet nectar.

He wasted no time and dived into his dessert. His tongue felt incredible to her. Misty reached out and ran her fingernails across his back. Tiny fissure like welts appeared on his dark brown skin. Kaiden bucked and pulled Misty closer to the edge of the bed,

Kaiden slithered his tongue lazily over the length of her slit. She stifled a shriek when he began to nibble on the tender insides of her lips. Syrup flowed freely from Misty. Soon she could feel as small puddle form while she dripped on the sheets. Kaiden let his skills ask everything he wanted to know.

Misty's' body recoiled in the struggle. His ingenious way of the tongue won. Misty gripped his shoulders tightly. She gasped for air while; her juices flooded onto his lips.

Breathless and shaken, Misty looked down at Kaiden. She ran her fingers through the sweaty, damp curls in his fade. Kaiden gazed up at Misty. He flicked his tongue across her engorged nubbin again.

Misty closed her eyes and leaned back on the bed. The back of her thighs tighten with anticipation. Whatever Kaiden chose to do, Misty had resolved to feel him. When she felt his fingertip brush lightly against her entrance, her thighs melted.

Kaiden gingerly played in Misty juices. His coated lips released warm air from into her most sensitive spot. After several strokes with his finger, Kaiden attempted to explore her inner depths. His finger met with defiant resistance.

Misty heard a sound similar to shredding foil. She kept her eyes closed. She felt Kaiden's' hand glazed over her hips. She trembled.

A cold gush of air ran the length of tummy. Misty did her best not to giggle. She felt firm hands grip the inside of her leg. The oiled sheet under had turned into a cold wetness.

The bed shifted. She resisted the urge to peek as Kaiden crawled atop of her. Misty gasped when the hot head of him pressed tightly against her open lips. She immediately clutched the sheets.

Kaiden pushed forward. Misty freely dripped her nectar, but her slit remained unopened. Kaiden rubbed his huge head against her. He pressed forward with more force.

Misty bit down harder on her lip. She winced from the pain that she had caused her. She had mentally prepared for Kaiden. Her body just was not cooperating.

Kaiden had been on his best behavior. He had made most of the right moves. His shaft raged with the need to feel Misty wrapped around him. At last, he let out a grunt of frustration.

"What's wrong Misty? I thought that you wanted this as much as I do." Kaiden asked.

Misty opened her eyes. Kaiden was very close to her face. She let go of the sheets and wrapped her arms around him in comforting him. His chiseled frame quaked with desire in her arms.

"Baby, this is part of the reason I didn't stay married long. I know it's tight, but I can't relax unless..." Misty said.

"Unless what, as long as you don't have to choke or hit me, tell me. I have seen a lot of stuff. I am a reformed porn addict. Just tell me baby and I'll do it." Kaiden said.

"Lie on your back, Kaiden."

Despite his size, Kaiden flipped on his back with speed. Misty shivered while; she drank in the sheer size of his maleness. It swung in the air and landed on his skim with a thud.

Misty crawled up to Kaiden's' face. He did not protest as she hoisted her leg over him. He cupped her ample cheeks and kissed between her open thighs. Misty sobbed as he resumed where he had left off earlier.

Kaiden pouted when Misty interrupted him. Until she reclaimed her seat on his lips backward. He spread the fleshy fold of her and once again began to suckle the sweet dew that waited for him. Kaiden had barely buried his face into her treasures when he gasped loudly.

His legs stiffened. Kaiden began to pat on the cheeks in his face with a nervous rhythm. His breaths became coveted bursts of air. Kaiden dug his fingers into Misty when she moved forward down the length of his body.

Now, that her plump hips no longer smothered him, he could breathe better. Kaiden stifled his moans for as long as he could. He turned his head towards her dresser. Kaiden's' eyes widen when he saw the reflection of him and Misty of the bed.

Even in the dim light, his eyes soaked up her sexiness. He ran his hands over the small of her back. Kaiden grimaced, and his toes curled inward. The temptation to rub his eyes had set in. He did not. Kaiden refused to miss even one second of Misty display of skills. Now, the only portion of his manhood that was evident was his sac.

CHAPTER SEVENTEEN

Thomas bent the corner of the central doorway. He came to a halt. Cameras and lights surrounded the entrance. His eyes enlarged.

Several news crews had amassed in a tight knot. Thomas was speechless as anchors shouted questions at him in a rush. He opened his mouth to ask for clarity of the situation. His voice was quickly drowned.

His band from the previous ten years had come together as one gigantic unit. The windows of the buildings vibrated as they marched into from the side of the building. His current students, in full uniform led the way. The students' from his current band had reached out to his former band members.

While the bodies made their procession into place, Thomas waited. After the 12th row of ten had bent the corner, he was in awe. By the time, the 50th row made their way in, Thomas had both of his cheeks in his hands. Thomas reeled from the shock of the 500 rich tributes.

He had come to work to plead the case of the students that worked hard to earn their trip. Thomas had left home ready for to fight for his kids. After all, that is how he saw them. This was his extended family, his brothers, and sisters.

Thomas remained quiet as the band played Luther Vandross version of "Never too much". He realized that people stared at him. Thomas moved his hands from his face and straightened his tie. Despite the shock, Thomas managed a meek smile.

He checked his watch; the meeting was due to start in less than half an hour. As much as this warmed his heart, he did not want to miss it. The band had to get to Lansing for the competition. Thomas began to get antsy.

Then the music died down. Thomas saw an opportunity to make a quick thank you speech and get to his meeting on time. Mrs. Yielder rolled up a chair and pointed to it. Thomas cut his eyes at her but sat down. He leaned over towards her and waved her closer. The band blared into a hearty rendition of "He's a Jolly Good Fellow".

"We are going to miss the meeting. This is a mandatory meeting specified by the Board of Directors. It is our last opportunity to get our point across. You got to get me out of here." Thomas said.

"Hush Thomas, you got to the meeting early. Now just hush." Mrs. Yielder said.

Nicole jumped up and down pointing to a limousine that pulled into the lot. The students continued to play. Scattered applause drifted in the morning air. Thomas strained to see past Nicole and the students.

Two well-dressed men exited the limousine. One of them carried a box while they walked towards Thomas. Thomas stood to his feet and shook their hands, once they were near. The Principle and all school staff had managed to clump behind the chair where Thomas had sat.

After several handshakes, Mrs. Yielder gave a bullhorn to the one of the men from the limousine. She put her hand on Thomas's shoulder. He looked at his watch once more and sat back down. Thomas hoisted his pants leg a bit and settled in.

"Thank you all for coming. I am Superintendent Bill, and my esteemed colleague is Rev. Wayne. We are happy to be here to present this award to Mr. Thomas Base at the request of his students. Mr. Base has been both a dedicated musician and an asset to his community. Because of his love for music, and continued cultivation of Fine Arts in the underprivileged areas of our great city, today we say thank you. This moment has been set aside to honor him. He has helped his students earn a spot in the Statewide Battle of the Bands Championship. Before we send them off to Lansing in buses so generously donated by the Sisters of "Oh They Going" driven by the fully licensed and Board approved Brothers of "Moving on up" company, we would like to present this award. This trophy is unique. I will step aside now so that Rev. Wayne can take part."

Thomas tried not laugh. The clergyman stepped forward and presented the box for Thomas to open. After he ripped, open the trophy box with his bare hands. Thomas pulled a magnificent sculpture from within.

"Hello everyone, it is both an honor and a pleasure to give this Thomas. The superintendent and I have known him for many years. While he has traveled extensively, Thomas has let the world know that he carried the love of music in his heart. He has remained loyal to the Detroit community and stayed local. It is because of his selfless sharing of his love of music and commitment to the growth of our inner city youth in the area of Fine Arts that we have gathered here.

Allow me to explain why this trophy is unique in nature. It has made several stops along the way to be here. The base is hand carved from ivory so that it stands on a pillar from the Motherland. The polished sticks are Black Onyx, a rare stone from the earth that is found within a band of colors. Finally, the inscribed nameplate, also hand carved, from an Oak Tree. The oak tree is well known for its strength and character. May the legacy of Mr. Thomas Base be recorded in our hearts, mind, and history." Rev. Wayne said.

"Mmmm hmm." Mrs. Yielder said.

A free round of applause thundered when Thomas stood up. He held the trophy firmly by his side. He paused. Thomas lifted the trophy over his head for all to see. The applause grew louder.

Thomas turned his head away for away and closed his eyes. Whether it was to say a quick prayer or hold back his emotions, one could only guess. Mrs. Yielder wrested the bullhorn from their guest and gave it to Thomas. He turned and hugged Mrs. Yielder before he spoke.

"I don't know what to say. I love you people so much. I want to thank you, my heavenly Father, to my mom, my whole family, my community, my co-workers, and to my students. This is not what I expected when I came to work today. I want to encourage every single student here to push for this day. I want the opportunity to present every single one of you with this same honor that you have given me today. We are going to Lansing kids! Thanks to the Sisters at "Oh yeah we going" and the Brothers at "Moving on up" we have a way. Not to rub it in your face but mama was right. Wherever there is a will, therein lies a way. We want to bring that State Championship Trophy to the heart of Michigan right here in Detroit. Meanwhile, I will display this one in case here for everyone to see, before I take it home and put it on my mantle. I want to see this every night when I go home. This is a physical reminder of your love and that the music never stops!"

Thomas handed the bullhorn to someone in the crown. He gazed at his trophy and smiled. He wished that his mom were there to share this moment. It would be a small token of appreciation for all of her sacrifices for him. Thomas excused himself and darted into the school.

Thomas moved so fast that he almost missed his office. He lunged across the desk and snatched the phone from the cradle. Carefully, he dialed the number to his dad. He held the phone with baited breath while he waited for his father to answer.

"Hello," James said.

"Hey Dad, I just got a trophy from the kids at school. I would have invited you, but I did not know. I..." Thomas said.

"I know. I am looking at it on the news right now. Get back out there and call me later." James interrupted.

"Oh, okay. Talk to you later dad."

"Son, before you hang up. I am proud of you. Your mother yakked on about that drum set for a month until it was under the tree. It was her idea. You know the best ones always were. Any way, I am sure that she is looking down at you and smiling about all this from up there. Now get off my phone, my forty getting warm yakking with you."

Thomas hung up. He rushed back down the corridor and burst through the doors. He had just stepped into the middle of a live interview. A golf cart came from over the sidewalk. It parked in front of Thomas.

One of Thomas's former students drove it. He yelled for Thomas to get in. Thomas reasoned that it would be easier to ride with trophy than walk it. He hopped in.

Thomas held the cup carefully on his lap to share it with everyone. When the cart pulled in front of the band, Thomas held it high. The driver drove slowly. Thomas rolled along while the band followed them and played a compilation of Motown's Greatest Hits. A mile later the crowd had grown to over a thousand people.

"Where are we going?" Thomas asked.

"To the church, the mother's cooked. If I don't get you there, they gone call my PO." the driver said.

"Your probation officer, Man, where did they find you at?"

"Leaving the county, some kid came up and said he'd give me ten bucks and feed me if I helped him get a golf cart."

Thomas' forehead wrinkled. He looked the young man up and down. Thomas' head swiveled around, and he still saw plenty of people. At last, Thomas looked at the steering column. He shook his head at the jumble of wires that hung down by the drivers' feet.

"Man, what were you in for and how did you get this thing?" Thomas asked.

"Grand theft auto, but I didn't do it, and I borrowed it. This is Detroit, what you want from me?" The man said.

"That's your story?"

"Yep"

"What kind of food did they promise?"

"Fried Chicken, Macaroni and cheese, greens, yams, and stuff."

"Speed up then."

BIG BODY BASE II

Author's Note

*I hope that you enjoyed this book. Stop by Inakat's House at
Inakat1.com or Inakat.com for other titles that you might like as
well or get a copy for your digital devices.
I look forward to penning future chapters to share with you.*

THIRD BASE
Coming Spring
2016

*Social Media
Inakat Publishing on FaceBook
Inakat1 on Twitter
Inakat on LinkdIn
Author Inakat on Google Plus*

BIG BODY BASE II

BIG BODY BASE II

www.ingramcontent.com/pod-product-compliance
Lightning Source LLC
Chambersburg PA
CBHW070801120626
46557CB00002B/681